THE
Parent Thief

MITRA MODARRESSI

ORCHARD BOOKS   NEW YORK

Orchard Books, 95 Madison Avenue, New York, NY 10016

Manufactured in the United States of America. Printed by Barton Press, Inc.
Bound by Horowitz/Rae. Book design by Mina Greenstein.
The text of this book is set in 14.5 point Aldus. The illustrations are watercolor
paintings reproduced in full color.   10 9 8 7 6 5 4 3 2 1

Library of Congress Cataloging-in-Publication Data
Modarressi, Mitra.
The parent thief / Mitra Modarressi.   p.   cm.
Summary: Bored with family vacations, Jack trades places with a
boy who lives on an island inhabited only by young people.
ISBN 0-531-09476-6.   ISBN 0-531-08776-X (lib. bdg.)
[1. Family life—Fiction. 2. Magic—Fiction.]   I. Title.
PZ7.M7137Par   1995   [E]—dc20   94-45916

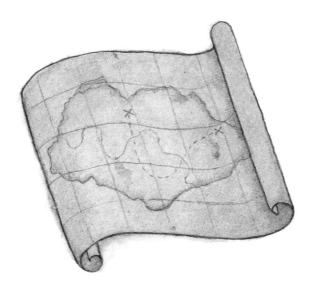

To Antonia and Jordin

JACK PARSLEY hated family vacations. When his mother told him the entire family was going on a boat trip, he threw a fit. He said, "Please, please, let me stay home. I can take care of myself." But his mother said no.

On board the S.S. *Mermaid*, his parents sunbathed and his twin sisters, Alice and Anna, played games. But Jack was bored hanging around with his family.

One night the ship's captain threw a party. Jack snuck out to the deck and leaned over the rail, scowling.

Suddenly Jack heard a noise. He turned and saw another little boy in the shadows. "Who are you?" he said.

"I'm Quinn," the boy replied. "You don't look very happy."

"No, I'm miserable and I wish I were a thousand miles away."

"That can be arranged," Quinn said. "I know a place a lot more fun than this."

"Where's that?" Jack asked.

"It's called Broomstick Island. I live there in a house all my own and there's no one but kids and we do whatever we like. Come and see for yourself."

"All right," Jack said.

Quinn stepped into something that
looked like a bathtub with a
striped balloon floating above. Jack
got in too, and they took off.

Jack loved flying through the night sky, and in no time they landed on a small island. Then Quinn took Jack around to meet the other kids. They were having a treasure hunt and invited Jack to join them.

It was almost midnight before he remembered his parents. "It's getting late," he told Quinn. "My parents will be wondering where I am."

Quinn said, "Oh, no, they won't. I'll show you." And he took Jack to a spyglass overlooking the harbor.

"S.S. *Mermaid!*" Quinn commanded, and magically the spyglass focused on Jack's parents dancing on deck. Jack could even hear the music.

"Boy," Jack said, "they're still at the same dumb party. I hate to go back."

Quinn said, "Then don't. I'll go instead and pretend to be you. I need a vacation anyhow."

"But you don't look anything like me!" Jack said.

"Maybe not," Quinn said, "but I can make your family think I'm you. I know a magic spell. I'll need something that belongs to you."

Jack found it hard to believe this would work, but he gave Quinn his hat anyway. "Only for a little while," he said.

"Just while they're on vacation," Quinn said. "You won't be sorry. You can stay at my house while I'm gone."

He showed Jack his house, which was exactly the right size for one person.
Then he took off in his balloon-boat.

Jack loved Broomstick Island. He played games with the other children and he went exploring.

He especially liked deep-sea fishing with his next-door neighbor, Clara.

When he felt like being alone, he read a book in the quiet of his very own home or cooked himself a feast.

One morning he remembered how his family baked cranberry muffins together for Sunday breakfast. He began to miss them. Their trip must be almost over, he thought.

He took a peek through the spyglass, but when he said, "S.S. *Mermaid*," he found the ship tied up to a dock, empty. The vacation had ended, but where was Quinn?

He told the spyglass, "The Parsley home." There, in Jack's house, was his family having cranberry muffins for breakfast! Quinn sat in Jack's chair, looking very much at home. Jack's father ruffled Quinn's hair just the way he always ruffled Jack's. The twins were nagging Quinn to fix their wagon, and twice Jack's mother called Quinn honey. The spell must have worked. Everyone was completely fooled.

Jack was horrified. He went to see his friend Clara. "Quinn's been away too long," he told her. "When do you think he's coming back? I need to get home to my family."

Clara said, "Oh, I don't think he'll be coming back. I'll bet he likes your family so much he's decided to stay for good."

Jack said, "But how will I ever get home?"

"I'll help," she told him.

Clara lent him her very own balloon-boat and set it on the right course.

When Jack reached home, he found Quinn out in the yard fixing the twins' wagon. Quinn said, "Jack! What a surprise!" He looked a little dismayed.

"You tricked me!" Jack said. "You planned to stay with my family forever, didn't you?"

Quinn said, "Well, I thought you were so miserable."

"Not *that* miserable," Jack said. "I would never give up my family."

"Oh, I'm sorry," Quinn said. "I must have misunderstood." He sighed. "Does this mean I have to leave?" he asked.

"It certainly does," Jack said.

Quinn handed over the hat. The spell was broken. Slowly he climbed into Clara's balloon-boat. "No hard feelings, I hope. Can we still be friends?" he asked.

"I suppose so," Jack said.

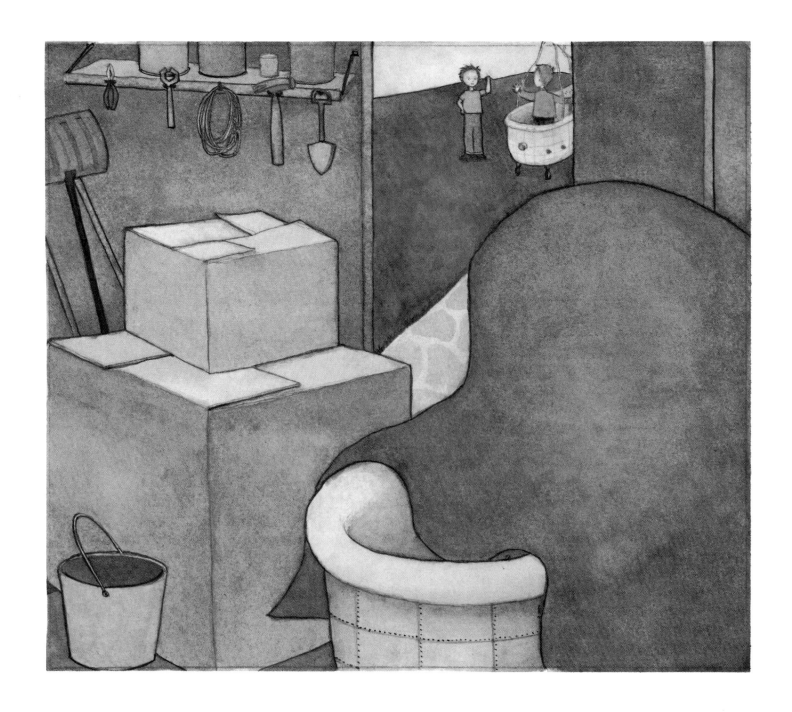

"I've hidden my own balloon-boat in the toolshed," Quinn told him. "Consider it a gift. That way you can always find me if you change your mind."

Then he took off, and Jack waved good-bye.

Jack did fly Quinn's balloon-boat quite often. Sometimes he even took his sisters along. But he never went too far away, and he was always home by bedtime.